MON BOY

Dino Destroyer • Ogre Outrage
Werewolf Wail

Sophia

ShooRayner

Find out more
about Monster Boy
at Shoo Rayner's
Wonderful Website
www.shoorayner.com

Published by Shoo Rayner

www.shoorayner.com

ISBN 978 1 908944 375

First published in Great Britain
2010 by ORCHARD BOOKS

This edition
Text and illustrations
© Shoo Rayner 2008-2017

A CIP catalogue record for this book is
available from the British Library.

Welcome to the Forest, where
The Ministry of Monsters
helps humans and monsters live side
by side in peace and harmony.

Connor O'Goyle
lives here too, with his gargoyle mum,
human dad and his flying dog, Trixie.
But Connor is no ordinary boy...

When monsters get out of control,
Connor's the one for the job.
He's half-monster, he's the Ministry's
Number One Agent,
and he's licensed to do things
no one else can do. He's...

Monster Boy!

MONSTER BOY

Book 1
Dino Destroyer

"Go fetch, girl!"
Connor yelled, throwing
a stick high into the air.

Trixie unfurled her wings
and zoomed after the stick.
As she snapped at it, her
wings stopped beating. She
froze in midair. Something
had scared her.

Her eyes opened
wide and her fur
stood up on end.
The stick tumbled
to the ground.

"You missed!"
Connor teased
his dog.

Trixie yelped and dropped like a brick. She fell into Connor's arms, knocking him flat on the ground.

"Oof! W-w-what the...?" Connor stammered.

A monstrous shape loomed against the skyline. A giant, scaly leg, with dagger-sharp claws smashed into the ground, exactly where Connor had been standing a few seconds before.

Boom!

The huge, deadly dinosaur lurched past him, tearing a path through the Forest as it headed off towards the town.

Trixie licked Connor's face and wagged her tail.

"Hey, stop it!" Connor complained.
Then he looked into his faithful friend's
eyes. "Thanks, Trix. I think you just
saved my life!"

An emergency alarm went off in Connor's pocket. He pulled out his MiPod and read the screen.

Mission Alert!

To: Monster Boy.
          Number One Agent

From: Mission Control
          Ministry of Monsters

Subject: Emergency in
          Beechnut Woods

Dinosaur (Tyrannosaurus Rex)
on the rampage. Please investigate
immediately.

Dinosaurs can be dangerous.

Approach with care.

Good luck!

M.O.M.

**THIS MESSAGE WILL
SELF-ERASE IN
FIFTEEN SECONDS**

Connor raced into the Pedal-O bike hire shop where he lived with his mum and dad.

PEDAL

Mum looked up from the mountain bike she was fixing. "What's up?" she asked calmly. She was used to Connor's monster emergencies.

"I need MB3 and fast," said Connor.

TOP SECRET

Mum wheeled the gleaming bike out of the secret store.

"I put some sandwiches and a bottle of water in the back," she told Connor. "Now, be careful, wear your helmet and give your mum a kiss before you go!"

"Oh, Mum!" Connor complained.

"Not now!"

Connor's mum was a Gargoyle, so
Connor was half-monster. His code-name
was Monster Boy. If anyone could look
after himself, Connor could.

Connor raced off
down the old railway
track that was now
a forest bike path.
Trixie leaned out of
her basket on the
handlebars.
She loved to
feel the wind
in her ears.

They were soon
in town, looking for
signs of the dinosaur.

"Wuff!" Trixie
pointed her nose
towards a terrifying
scene of devastation.

A large office building
crumbled before their eyes.
Through the clouds of dust, they
saw giant, powerful jaws open wide.
Enormous teeth sunk into the side of
the building. The walls collapsed in a
shower of bricks and concrete.

"Excuse me!" Connor called out to a man in a bright yellow builder's helmet. "Have you seen a dinosaur round here?"

"No dinosaurs here, mate," the man called back. "Only that old monster there." He pointed to the demolition machine that soared high above them. Its mechanical jaws tore into the building, biting out the window frames and chomping up the roof tiles.

Something was written on the machine's long, extending arm. Connor screwed up his eyes. "Raze-it Demolition Corporation," he read aloud.

"Aye," said the man. "That's us. Now, you'd better move along. It's dangerous round here."

MiPOD MONSTER IDENTIFIER PROGRAM

MONSTER

Tyrannosaurus Rex

Distinguishing Features:
Sharp teeth and claws.

Preferred habitat:
Pre-historic Earth.

Essential Information:
A few dinosaurs survive in the forest. Sadly, there is only one Tyrannosaurus Rex left. He is happy as long as he lets off steam once in a while, but he often gets bored and lonely.

Danger Rating: 5

On the footbridge over the main road, Connor saw what he had most feared. The dinosaur roared as cars skidded and crashed into each other. Frightened drivers and passengers ran for their lives. "T-Rex, stop!" Connor shouted.

The huge beast turned its giant head and glared back at him. It picked up an abandoned car and ripped it in half with its teeth. "You gonna make me?" T-Rex roared.

T-Rex clawed open the side of a truck and scrunched up a bus as if it were made of cardboard. In no time, the road looked like a scrap yard.

Connor had to stop T-Rex before he did more damage. But how?

Connor's MiPod pinged again. It was a message from his dad, Gary O'Goyle, the world-famous Mountain Bike Champion. Dad always sent messages at the most unhelpful times!

HOLLYWOOD

Hi son,
Having a great time at the
Hollywood Celebrity Mountain
Bike Race.
Here's a picture of me and
Cowboy Jim, the rodeo star.
I got his autograph for you!

Lots of love,
Dad

"Cowboy Jim!"
Connor whooped.
"That gives me an
idea. Thanks, Dad!"

"Ready?" Connor asked
his faithful pet. Trixie
wagged her tail and
snuffed her nose in a
sneeze of joy. She loved
chasing monsters!

Connor aimed the bike handlebars at the dinosaur's legs. He flipped open the lid of his bell and pressed the red launch button. "Fire!"

Two missiles streaked out of the
front suspension forks. Each missile
spun out a fine thread behind it. The
thread was a top secret material.
Made from a giant, monster spider's
web, it was ten times stronger than
steel but felt as soft as silk.

Monster Bike Info
MB3

MB3 is a capture bike. It has many attachments to suit the capture of monsters.

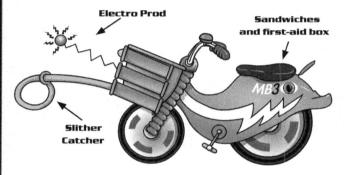

Electro Prod

Sandwiches and first-aid box

Slither Catcher

MB3 Monster Missiles are radio-controlled from the handlebars.

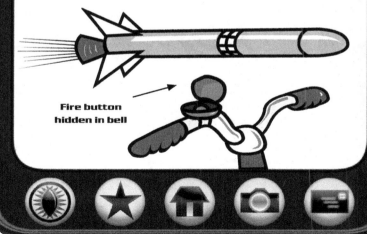

Fire button hidden in bell

Connor guided the missiles using the handlebars as controllers.

The missiles wrapped the thread round and round T-Rex's legs.

Trixie knew what to do. She flew around the dinosaur's head to distract him. He snapped his powerful jaws and lunged at her. The thread wound tighter and tighter around his legs.

One final snap at the brave little
dog made the lumbering beast lose
his balance. T-Rex came crashing
to the ground. Soon the monster
lay silent and helpless in the
middle of the road.

Connor patted his happy, tail-wagging
friend. "Nice work, Trix!"

Connor stood over
the monster and stared
into its giant yellow
eyes. "Now, have you
quite finished, T-Rex?"
Connor sighed.

The dinosaur snorted and slumped his huge head on the ground – defeated by a boy and his dog!

But Connor was half monster himself. He understood that monsters have feelings too.

"You can't go round eating cars whenever you feel like it." Connor whispered to the beast.

Connor paused for a moment while
he collected his thoughts.
Then he smiled and said,
"I've had an idea you
just might be
interested in."

"So where's the dinosaur now?" asked Connor's Mum as they cycled into town to do the weekly shop.

"You'll see in a minute," Connor told her, with a twinkle in his eye.

Mum knew that he must have come
up with one of his monster solutions.
Connor liked to help monsters with
their problems.

Connor's breaks squealed. "There!"
he said, pointing at the demolition site.

Danger!
Demolition
Site

T-Rex and the enormous wrecking machine moved together in a dance of destruction. Together they ripped and slashed and chomped and bashed their way through the office building. It was almost beautiful to watch.

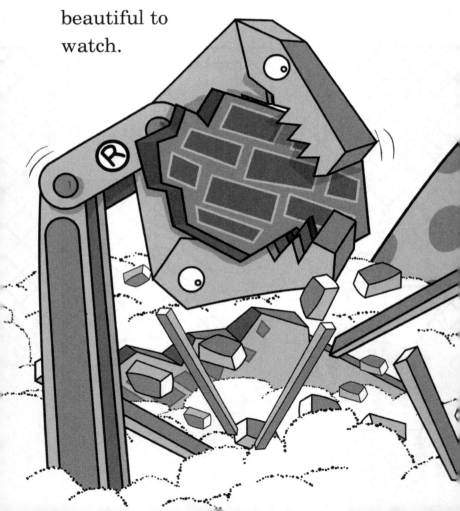

The man in the
yellow helmet
came up and shook
Connor's hand.
"T-Rex is the best
worker we've ever
had," he laughed.

41

"They look so happy together," Mum said, as she watched the dinosaur and the wrecking machine work in perfect harmony.

Connor smiled. "Poor old T-Rex — all he needed was someone like him to play with!"

"Wuff!" Trixie had found a piece of wood. She dropped it at Connor's feet.

Connor laughed. "Want to play too, Trix?" He picked up the stick and threw it high into the sky.

"Go fetch, girl!"

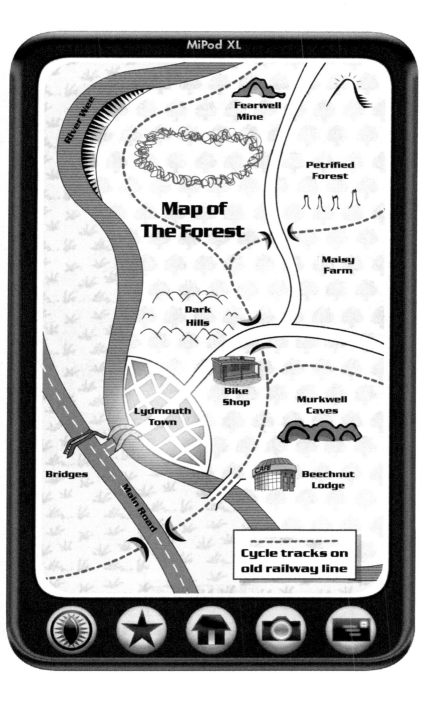

Book 2
Mummy Menace

"That's disgusting!"
Connor gasped.

Trixie had
found a toilet
roll in the bushes.
She was playing
with it like a toy.

47

"You don't know where it's been or where it's come from," Connor called to his dog. "It's probably full of germs!"

Trixie didn't mind.
She was having fun.
It was only a toilet roll!

As she tossed it in the air, the end
came loose and began to unwind.
She was soon tangled up in the paper.

It's not like the soft stuff we have at home, Trixie thought, as she unfurled her wings.

"No!" Connor called. "Trixie! Come back right now!"

It was too late. Trixie flapped her wings and swooped around Connor's head. The toilet paper streamed behind her like a ribbon, creating pretty shapes in the air.

Connor sighed and sat down on a tree stump. There was nothing to do but wait. Trixie was having a wonderful time.

Connor's Mipod beeped in his pocket. It was a message from the Ministry of Monsters.

Mission Alert!

To:	Monster Boy. Number One Agent
From:	Mission Control Ministry of Monsters
Subject:	Someone or something has been taking all the paper from our public toilets.

Suspicious activity has been reported near the loos at the Tinkle Falls Café. Please investigate immediately.

Good luck!

M.O.M.

**THIS MESSAGE WILL
SELF-ERASE IN
FIFTEEN SECONDS**

"I've got a job," Connor told his mum, as he rushed into the Pedal-O bike shop where they lived. "I'll need MB1 and lots of sandwiches."

Mum pressed a button to open the
hidden workshop where she looked
after Connor's top secret Monster
Bikes. MB1 was his all-purpose
patrol bike.

Five minutes
later, Connor was
ready and Mum
had checked
MB1 over.

"All systems are working fine
and I've packed orange juice and
sandwiches," she said.

"Thanks, Mum." Connor swung his leg over the seat and lifted Trixie into her basket.

Mum gave Connor a little hug. "Please be careful," she said. "I do worry about you!"

"Oh, *Mum!*" Connor groaned, as he pedalled off. "I'll be fine. Stop worrying."

Connor's mum was a Gargoyle, so Connor was half monster. His code-name was Monster Boy. If anyone could look after himself, Connor could.

Tinkle Falls was a tiny waterfall in the gently flowing River Wee. It was a favourite place for picnickers, with a small café, a children's play area and public toilets.

Connor leaned MB1 against a tree
and switched on the monster detector.
Then he sat down on the grass and
began to eat his sandwiches.

From behind his sunglasses he
surveyed the scene and tried to look
like any other kid.

Suddenly, someone screamed.
Someone else shouted.

A moving mountain of toilet rolls ran
from the toilets and stumbled off into
the woods.

A red light flashed on MB1's control panel.

"Monster alert!" he told Trixie. "Let's get going."

Connor's Mipod pinged again. It was a message from his dad, Gary O'Goyle, the world famous Mountain Bike Champion. His dad always sent messages at the most unhelpful moments!

Hi Son,

Having a great time in Egypt at the Valley of the Kings International Mountain Bike Championships. There are no mountains. We have to ride up and down the Pyramids instead!

Lots of love

Dad

"The pyramids!" Connor muttered under his breath. Suddenly he had an idea of what he might be dealing with.

Connor leaped onto MB1 and raced off into the woods.

Trixie barked from her basket and pointed her nose at something on the ground. Trixie loved chasing monsters.

"Toilet paper!" Connor whispered. "Well done, Trix. We're on the right track."

It was dark in the woods. Connor switched on the night-vision camera. He turned the handlebar to and fro. A trail of small white sheets glowed on the control panel screen.

"This way," Connor said. Now and then, Connor caught a glimpse of the monster as they followed the trail of paper through the woods.

Trixie growled. The fur stood up on her back. Connor knew what that meant. The monster must be close.

Connor switched the camera to monster-detector vision. The glowing outline of a body showed up on the screen.

"He's just behind that bush," Connor whispered.

Connor pedalled MB1 up to full speed. He raced across the clearing, expertly threw the bike into a half-brake slide and skidded around the back of the bush, taking the monster by surprise.

"Wah!" The monster leaped into the air tossing toilet rolls in all directions.

A dusty cloud of fluttery objects flew into Connor's face. He couldn't breathe. He took his hands off the brakes to brush away the crawling, clinging, things.

The bike wobbled. Connor lost his balance. He never saw the tree. He fell off MB1 with a bump!

There was a loud bang, then a hiss as the rescue-beacon balloon filled with gas and floated upwards on its cord. The contents of the first aid kit spilled out on the ground.

Monster Bike Info

MB3

MB1 is fitted out with everything that Connor might need on a long Monster Mission.

Control Panel

Monster Detectors

Sandwiches and first-aid box in equipment bays

The ESPxl Monster Detector Screen can even identify monsters in the dark!

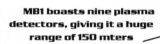

MB1 boasts nine plasma detectors, giving it a huge range of 150 mters

Connor squinted through the pain. "I knew it!" he yelped. "You're a Mummy. Why have you been stealing all the toilet paper?"

"Moths," said the Mummy.

"Moths?!"
Connor squeaked.

"They've been eating my bandages," the Mummy explained. "I can't be seen in public looking like this!"

Connor screwed up his eyes and took a good look at the Mummy. His bandages were chewed to bits. Maggots crawled among the tattered remains. The Mummy was right - he looked terrible.

"You frightened my moths," the Mummy continued. "That's why they flew in your face."

Connor spat a moth from his mouth. "Eugh! But why did you steal the toilet paper? He asked.

"It's all I could get to patch myself up," the Mummy told him. "I've tried electrical tape, sellotape, even police crime-scene tape. The moths chew through everything. I wish I could get nice bandages like this."

Connor realised that the Mummy was gently strapping his leg with a bandage from the first aid kit.

"You'll be okay," said the Mummy, "but your leg might be sore for a while"

In the distance, Connor heard the sound of an ambulance responding to his emergency beacon. He knew he would be safe now.

MiPOD MONSTER IDENTIFIER PROGRAM

MONSTER	
Mummy	

Distinguishing Features:

Fingers and toes are tied on in case they break and fall off!

Preferred habitat:

Secret passages and triangular buildings.

Essential Information:

Mummies are not very clever. Most of their brains were scooped out through their noses. The ancient Egyptians did not have toilet paper. They probably used a wet sponge on a stick or they used a seashell as a scraper!

Danger Rating: 1

Six weeks later, Mum rode Connor to the hospital in the back of the trailer bike. Connor's leg had mended. It was time to have the plaster taken off.

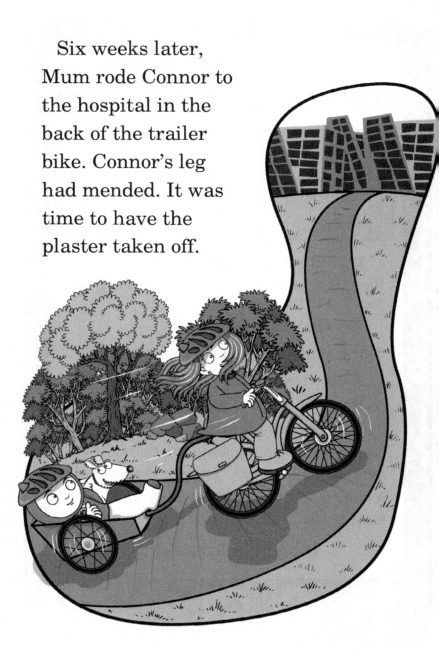

A tall figure loomed into the waiting room and called their name.

It was the Mummy! His bandages were clean and fresh and perfectly wrapped.

In the treatment room, the Mummy began gently and carefully cutting off Connor's plaster.

X-RAY

"I should thank you for saving my son's life!" Mum gushed.

The Mummy smiled. "Oh I only looked after Connor until the ambulance came. It's my fault he had the accident in the first place. Anyway, I have to thank Connor for saving me!"

Mum raised an eyebrow and looked at Connor.

"I told the doctors about the Mummy when they set my leg in plaster," Connor explained. "They were really impressed with his bandaging and offered him a job."

"I hope they pay you properly?" Mum asked. "People take monsters for granted, you know?"

The Mummy smiled. "They pay me very well. I get fresh bandages every week and a spray to keep the moths and maggots away. It's wonderful – now I can help people instead of scaring them and stealing their toilet paper."

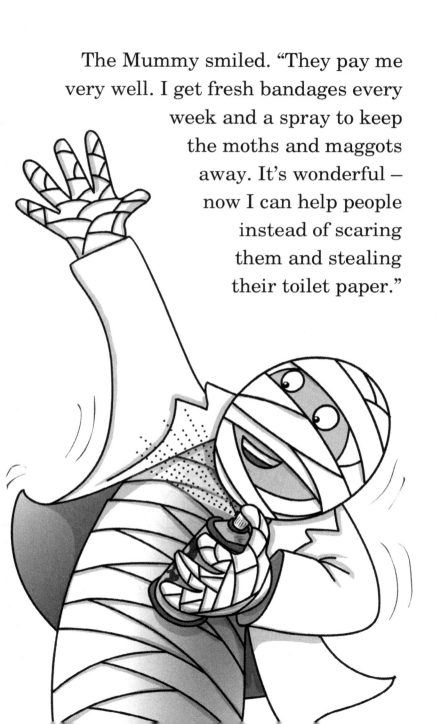

"A perfect monster solution," Connor smiled. Then he screwed his face up with a look of excuciating pain. "There's something I have to ask you," he said.

"You can ask me anything you like," said the Mummy.

"Where's the toilet?" said Connor.

Book 3
Ogre Outrage

"This bike is pathetic!" Connor moaned. MB2 was a state of the art, carbon-fibre, monocot, power-assisted wonder bike – but it was a little bit small.

"It's really good in tight places," Connor's mum explained, patiently. Connor's mum was the mechanic at the Pedal-O bike hire shop, where she looked after Connor's amazing top-secret Monster Bikes.

Connor's dog, Trixie, sniffed the wheels. "There's no room for Trixie," Connor grumbled.

Mum pulled open the hatch at the back. "Yes there is."

"There's no room for sandwiches!" Connor was not happy with the new bike.

"I've made you nice, small sandwiches," Mum smiled.

"They're not proper sandwiches!"
Connor moaned.

"They fit perfectly under the saddle."
said Mum. "Anyway, you should be
grateful to have any sandwiches at all.
Bread has become hard to get since the
baker left town."

Just then, Connor's MiPod bleeped.

MiPod XL

Mission Alert!

To:	Monster Boy
	Number One Agent
From:	Mission Control
	Ministry of Monsters
Subject:	An Ogre is on the
	rampage in
	Dark Hills.

He's not getting his daily bread
and it's making him grumpy.

Please investigate immediately.
Be careful. He's very grumpy.

Good luck!
M.O.M

THIS MESSAGE WILL

SELF-ERASE IN

FIFTEEN SECONDS

"I know how the Ogre feels," Connor muttered, as he climbed into the saddle of MB2.

"Wait a second." Mum pressed a button on the control panel. "This is the really good bit." A small electronic screen popped up on the handlebars. "Satellite Navigation!" she announced.

Connor perked up. "Wow! That's amazing! Come on Trix, get your helmet on. We can try it out right now!"

The Sat Nav unit plotted a route to the Dark Hills.

Dark Hills

Mission Alert!
Mipod Info
The Dark Hills

Dark Hills were the site of ancient iron mining over 1000 years ago.

Magnetic forces in the iron are powerful enough to make clocks run slow and affect electronic equipment. Radios in the area can only pick up Russian pop music stations.

M.O.M.

"It will be a good test," Connor's mum said. "But make sure you stick to the path and follow the route on the Sat Nav."

She looked nervous as she waved goodbye to her son. Not everyone who went to the Dark Hills came out again!

"Don't worry, Mum, I'll be fine!" Connor yelled as he pedalled off.

Connor's mum was a Gargoyle, so Connor was half monster himself. His code-name was Monster Boy. If anyone could look after himself, Connor could.

The Dark Hills looked like their name sounded. Hundreds of small, dark red hills created a tangled web of narrow paths between them.

Trixie leaned out of her hatch, took in the view and growled a warning.

"The Sat Nav says to go straight ahead. We can't get lost." Connor reassured her. "Hold on tight. Here we go!"

Mum was right. In the tight
pathways between the hills,
MB2 steered like a dream.

Soon, they were right in the
middle of the maze of hills.
Haven't we passed that tree before!
Connor wondered.

A minute later he skidded to a halt. "That's the third time we've passed that tree," Connor said, as he tapped the Sat Nav. The map swung round on the screen and pointed in a different direction.

"Oh great! We're lost!"

Connor's Mipod beeped. At least that was working.

"It's a message from Dad!" said Connor.

Connor's dad was Gary O'Goyle, the world famous Mountain Bike Champion. He always sent messages at the most unhelpful times.

Hi Son,

I'm having a great time at the All Ireland Mountain Bike Challenge. Great to be back home, staying with your Granny. She sends her love.
Here's a picture of us having a picnic.

Lots of love …

Dad

"Oh great!" said Connor. "Granny gives him proper sandwiches! There's no bread shortage there!"

Trixie barked and stared into the distance. She'd heard something.

Soon Connor heard it too. A slow dragging thump of heavy feet on the soft ground. Then a rasping, booming voice filled the air.

Fee! Fi! Fo! Fum! I smell the blood of an Englishman! Be he alive or be he dead, I'll grind his bones to make my bread!

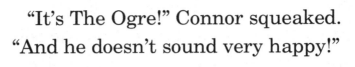

"It's The Ogre!" Connor squeaked. "And he doesn't sound very happy!"

Connor slammed MB2 into power-assist mode and screeched off down the path, spraying mud and leaves behind him.

Connor felt the thud of heavy footsteps through the ultra-light, carbon-fibre bike frame. The Sat Nav map swung round in manic circles. It was useless. Connor had no idea which way to go!

"Raaar!" The Ogre loomed out of nowhere, blocking the path.

He was behind me a second ago, Connor thought as he slammed the bike into a half-brake skid.

However scared he was, Connor couldn't help but be impressed with the way the bike handled!

Monster Bike Info
MB2

The small carbon fibre body of MB2 works best in narrow and twisty environments.

Pop-up Satelite Navigation System

Backpack suitable for small dog & very small sandwiches

Ultra lightweight titanium Wheels

Ultra lightweight carbon fibre body

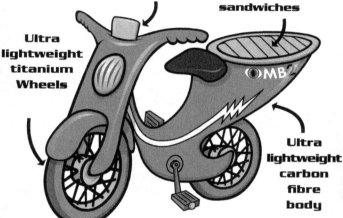

The MB2 Sat Nav shows the current location by using up to seven orbiting satellites. It can be confused by strong magnetic forces.

Pop-up Sat Nav

The Ogre waved a large,
knobbly club above his large
knobbly head. His teeth were
broken and green with scum.
Stiff, bristly hairs
poked out of his ears.
His nostrils flared in
his piggy-like snout.

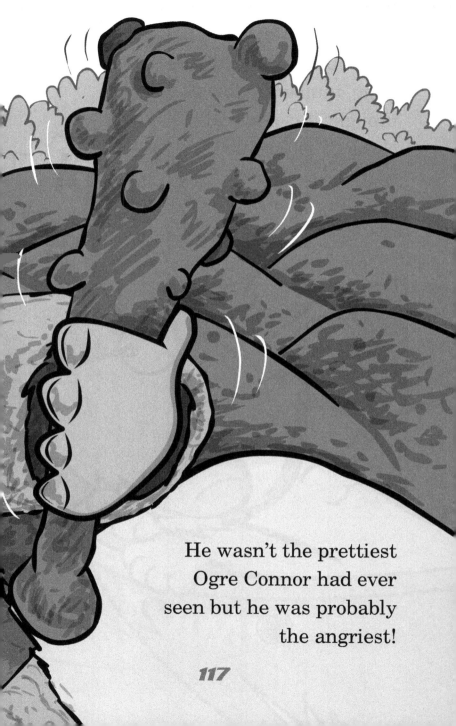

He wasn't the prettiest
Ogre Connor had ever
seen but he was probably
the angriest!

117

Trixie barked wildly as the Ogre's huge, lumbering footsteps brought it closer and closer. The air filled with it's constant, growling chant.

Connor shifted into fifteenth gear. The pedals stiffened. His calf muscles tensed. He gripped the handlebars tightly, slipping and sliding his amazing new bike through ninety degree turns. He was accelerating faster than any other bike could have managed on the pathways of the lonely Dark Hills.

But it was no use. He could feel
the Ogre's hand almost on him. He
was exhausted. His aching body was
powerless. The path was too steep.
He was finished!

"Fee! Fi! Fo! Fum! I smell the blood of an Englishman!" the Ogre laughed, showering Connor in yellow spit and foul breath.

"Be he alive or be he dead, I'll grind his bones to..."

An idea popped into Connor's head.
"Actually," he said. "I'm half Irish."

"Huh!" The Ogre looked confused.

"Yeah..." Connor tried playing it cool. "...and my mum's a Gargoyle!"

"Garrr–goyle!" the Ogre yelped.
"Gargoyle taste disgusting."
He let go of Connor as if he were
poison. Then he looked at Trixie and
smiled. "Dog is good!"

Trixie unfurled her wings and flew to the top of a tree.

"Huh!" the Ogre grumbled. "Not a proper Dog!"

"Would you like to share my sandwiches?" Connor asked, casually.

"Mmmm!" the Ogre smiled. "Bread!"

MiPOD MONSTER IDENTIFIER PROGRAM

MONSTER

OGRE

Distinguishing Features:
Knobbly head, hairy ears, filthy teeth.

Preferred habitat:
Caves.

Essential Information:
Ogres are all noise and no action. However, they are keen to keep up their fearsome reputation so they might pretend to eat you. Ogres like to live quietly in their caves cooking, cleaning and sewing interesting clothes.

They do not like to be disturbed.

Danger Rating: 4

"So which do you prefer?" Connor asked as he handed the Ogre one of his tiny sandwiches. "Grinding bones or making bread?"

"Mmmmm! Bread!" the Ogre growled
happily, as he popped the tiny sandwich
into his huge, dribbling mouth.
"Hmmmm – good!"

"If you show me the way home,"
Connor bargained, "I've had an idea
that just might interest you."

A few weeks later, Connor and his mum were finishing their shopping in the supermarket.

"I wonder if they've got any bread for your sandwiches yet?" said Mum.

"M-m-m-m! Monster bread!" Connor roared in an Ogre-ish sort of way. He pointed to a display of giant-sized loaves of bread.

There was an enormous, cardboard cut-out of the Ogre with a sign that read:

NEW!
Monster Bread
Baked fresh
every day by
your local,
friendly Ogre

Mum raised her eyebrows. "You'd need a much bigger bike if you had sandwiches that size," she joked.

Connor smiled sweetly. "It's funny you should say that... I've been thinking for a while that I really could do with a much bigger bike!"

If you enjoyed this book,
then learn to draw Connor and Trixie,
and hundreds of other things too, with
Shoo Rayner's famous,
award-winning YouTube videos.

Find out more about Monster Boy
and all Shoo's other books
and get masks and colour-in sheets
at www.shoorayner.com

Lightning Source UK Ltd.
Milton Keynes UK
UKOW06f2150031117
312085UK00006B/442/P